Tadpoles

My Auntie Susan

Crabtree Publishing Company
www.crabtreebooks.com
1-800-387-7650

PMB 16A, 350 Fifth Ave.
Suite 3308,
New York, NY

616 Welland Ave.
St. Catharines, ON
L2M 5V6

Published by Crabtree Publishing in 2008

Series Editor: Jackie Hamley
Editor: Melanie Palmer
Series Advisor: Dr. Hilary Minns
Series Designer: Peter Scoulding
Proofreader: Reagan Miller

First published in 2007
by Franklin Watts
(A division of Hachette Children's Books)

Printed in the U.S.A.—CG

For Auntie Sue – S.M.B.

Library and Archives Canada Cataloguing in Publication

Bird, Sheila
My Auntie Susan / Sheila May Bird ;
Daniel Postgate, illustrator.

(Tadpoles)
ISBN 978-0-7787-3858-9 (bound).
--ISBN 978-0-7787-3889-3 (pbk.)

1. Readers (Primary). 2. Readers--
Personality. I. Postgate, Daniel II. Title. III. Series:
Tadpoles (St. Catharines, Ont.)

PE1117.T33 2008l 428.6 C2007-907413-8

Library of Congress Cataloging-in-Publication Data

Bird, Sheila.
My Auntie Susan / by Sheila May Bird ;
illustrated by Daniel Postgate.
p. cm. -- (Tadpoles)
Summary: The narrator lists in simple rhyming text some of the great things about Auntie Susan, who wears a long scarf and likes to cook and bake.
ISBN-13: 978-0-7787-3858-9 (reinforced lib. bdg.)
ISBN-10: 0-7787-3858-2 (reinforced lib. bdg.)
ISBN-13: 978-0-7787-3889-3 (pbk.)
ISBN-10: 0-7787-3889-2 (pbk.)
[1. Stories in rhyme. 2. Aunts--Fiction.] I. Postgate, Daniel, ill. II. Title. III. Series.

PZ8.3.B5318My 2008
[E]--dc22

2007049223

My Auntie Susan

by Sheila May Bird

Illustrated by Daniel Postgate

Crabtree Publishing Company

www.crabtreebooks.com

Sheila May Bird

"I like writing, reading too, and eating cake with Auntie Sue."

Daniel Postgate

"I have a few unusual relatives, like my brother, Kevan. He lives in a hut in India and spends his time writing poetry."

My Auntie Susan – what is she like?

She wears a top hat
and she rides on a bike.

She has lines on her face, but I don't think she's old.

She wears a long scarf, even when it's not cold.

She likes to cook,
she likes to bake.

Her favorite food is upside-down cake.

Sometimes she gets in a bit of a muddle.

That's when she needs a bit of a cuddle.

I like my Auntie, as
I'm sure you can see ...

Because Auntie Susan is a lot like me!

Notes for adults

TADPOLES are structured to provide support for early readers. The stories may also be used by adults for sharing with young children.

Starting to read alone can be daunting. **TADPOLES** help by providing visual support and repeating high frequency words and phrases. These books will both develop confidence and encourage reading and rereading for pleasure.

If you are reading this book with a child, here are a few suggestions:

1. Make reading fun! Choose a time to read when you and the child are relaxed and have time to share the story.
2. Talk about the story before you start reading. Look at the cover and the blurb. What might the story be about? Why might the child like it?
3. Encourage the child to reread the story, and to retell the story in their own words, using the illustrations to remind them what has happened.
4. Discuss the story and see if the child can relate it to their own experiences, or perhaps compare it to another story they know.
5. Give praise! Children learn best in a positive environment.

If you enjoyed this book, why not try another TADPOLES story?

At the End of the Garden
9780778738503 RLB
9780778738817 PB

Bad Luck, Lucy!
9780778738510 RLB
9780778738824 PB

Ben and the Big Balloon
9780778738602 RLB
9780778738916 PB

Crabby Gabby
9780778738527 RLB
9780778738831 PB

Five Teddy Bears
9780778738534 RLB
9780778738848 PB

I'm Taller Than You!
9780778738541 RLB
9780778738855 PB

Leo's New Pet
9780778738558 RLB
9780778738862 PB

Little Troll
9780778738565 RLB
9780778738879 PB

Mop Top
9780778738572 RLB
9780778738886 PB

My Auntie Susan
9780778738589 RLB
9780778738893 PB

My Big, New Bed
9780778738596 RLB
9780778738909 PB

Pirate Pete
9780778738619 RLB
9780778738923 PB

Runny Honey
9780778738626 RLB
9780778738930 PB

Sammy's Secret
9780778738633 RLB
9780778738947 PB

Sam's Sunflower
9780778738640 RLB
9780778738954 PB